KU-664-693

Mog and Bunny

Judith Kerr

COLLINS

For Lucy and Alexander

William Collins Sons & Co Ltd
London · Glasgow · Sydney · Auckland
Toronto · Johannesburg

First published by William Collins Sons & Co Ltd 1988
© text and illustrations Kerr-Kneale Productions Ltd 1988
Third impression 1988
British Library Cataloguing in Publication Data

Kerr, Judith
Mog and Bunny.
I. Title
823'.914[J]   PZ7

ISBN 0-00-195595-0

All rights reserved. No part of this
publication may be reproduced, stored
in a retrieval system, or transmitted,
in any form or by any means, electronic,
mechanical, photocopying, recording or
otherwise, without the prior permission
of William Collins Sons & Co Ltd,
8 Grafton Street, London W1X 3LA.

Printed and bound in Great Britain
by William Collins Sons & Co Ltd, Glasgow

105773

LIBRARY
WESTMINSTER COLLEGE
OXFORD. OX2 9AT

KERR,
MOG AND BUNNY
105773 06   J823.91 KER

105773

WESTMINSTER COLLEGE
LIBRARY

20 OCT 1989   2 2 MAR 1990   2 8 JAN 1992   1 JUN

                - 3 MAY 1990   23 SEP 91
                                2 3 APR 1991
0 6 NOV 1989   - 6 JUN 1990

2 1 FEB 1990   1 7 DEC 1991

1 3 MAR 1990   2 7 JUN 1990 MAY 1991

                29. JUN 90   - 8 MAY 1991
2 3 MAR 1990   1 4 DEC 1990   8 MAY 1992
2 8 MAR 1990   11. JUN 92
- 6 APR 1990   2 7   1 4 DEC 1992

If found please return to the College in Oxford

One day Mog got a present.
"Here you are, Mog," said Nicky.
"This is for you. It's called Bunny."

Mog liked Bunny.

She carried him about.

She played with him . . .

and played with him . . .

and played . . .

and played . . .

and played with him.

He was her best thing.

When Mog came to have her supper, Bunny came too.

Sometimes Mog thought Bunny would like a drink.

But Bunny wasn't very
good at drinking.
"Oh dear," said Debbie.
"Look where Bunny's got to."

And she put him on the radiator to dry.

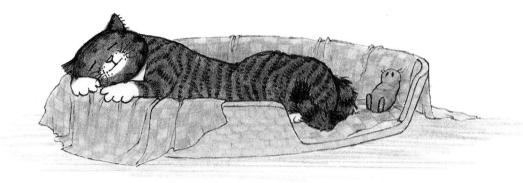

At night Bunny slept with Mog in her basket.

During the day,
when Mog was busy,
she always put Bunny
somewhere nice.
You never knew where
Bunny would get to.

Sometimes Bunny liked to be quiet and cosy,

and sometimes he liked to be where there was a lot going on.

Mr and Mrs Thomas didn't understand this.
They didn't say, "Look where Bunny's got to."
They shouted, "Yukk!"

They yelled, "Arrgh! What a horrible, dirty thing!"

And they threatened to throw Bunny away in the dustbin.

One day Mr Thomas said, "Let's have supper in the garden."

Everyone helped to carry things out of the house.

It was a lovely supper.

But suddenly . . .

. . . there was a crash of thunder and it poured with rain.

"Quick! Inside!" shouted Mrs Thomas. "It's bedtime anyway."

"Where's Mog?" said Debbie.
"I expect she's keeping dry
under a bush," said Mrs Thomas.
"She'll come in later."

In the middle of
the night, Debbie
and Nicky woke up.
Mog hadn't come in
and it was still
pouring with rain.
"Let's go and find her,"
said Debbie.

It was very dark in the garden.
They shouted, "Mog! Where are you, Mog?"
But nothing happened.

Then they heard a meow.
"There she is!" shouted Nicky.
"Come on, Mog! Come inside!"
But Mog just went on sitting in the rain.

It was . . .

dripping . . .

off her nose.

"What's the matter, Mog?" said Debbie.
Then she said, "Oh dear! Look where Bunny's got to."

Nicky picked Bunny up
and showed him to Mog.
"It's all right, Mog," he said.
"We've set Bunny free.
You can come inside now."

Then they carried Bunny through the dark garden . . .

and through the house . . .

and they put him on the radiator to dry.

Then they all had a big sleep.

In the morning they told Mrs Thomas what had happened,
and how Mog had stayed with Bunny in the dark and the rain.

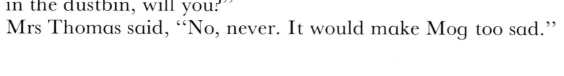

Debbie said, "You won't really throw Bunny away
in the dustbin, will you?"
Mrs Thomas said, "No, never. It would make Mog too sad."

Then she sighed and said,
"Perhaps he's not quite so
horrible, now he's been
washed by the rain."
They all looked on the radiator.

But this is where Bunny had got to.